ANIMALS AND THEIR BABIES

DOGS AND PUPPIES

By Annabelle Lynch

Contents

W

FRANKLIN WATTS

LONDON • SYDNEY

GROWING INSIDE

This dog has babies growing in her **tummy.**

2

The dog's tummy gets bigger and bigger as her puppies grow!

After about 60 days, the puppies are ready to be born.

3

GIVING BIRTH

A mother dog finds somewhere safe and warm to have her **babies.**

The mother dog licks her
newborn puppies clean.
She stays close to keep
them warm.

Snuggle up!

SEEING AND HEARING

When they are born, puppies cannot see or hear. Their eyes and ears stay closed.

Puppies begin to see and hear when they are about two weeks old.

Puppies stay close together so they are safe.

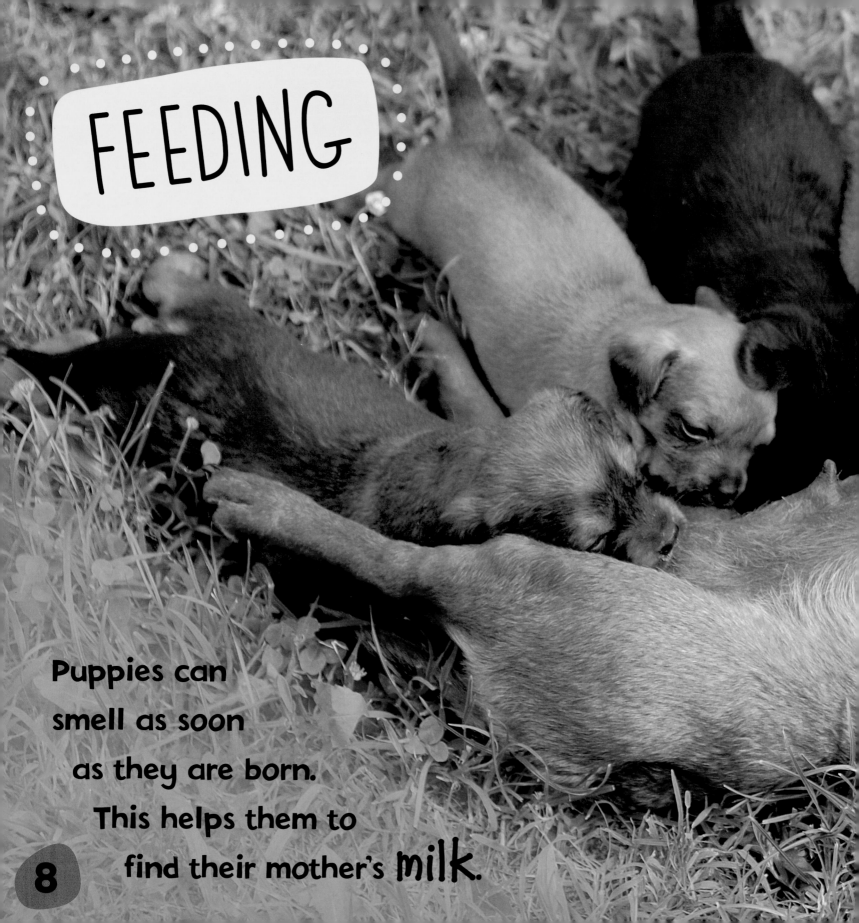

FEEDING

Puppies can smell as soon as they are born. This helps them to find their mother's milk.

8

Puppies suck the milk out of their mother's **teats**.

They feed only on their mother's milk until they are about **four weeks** old.

MOVING

Puppies learn to walk when they are about three weeks old.

They are a bit **wobbly** at first!

Now puppies can move around, they love to find out more about the world.

Sometimes they get a bit tired though!

GROWING TEETH

When they are two or three weeks old, puppies start growing their first teeth. These teeth are small but very **sharp!**

Now puppies can start eating solid food. They still drink their mother's milk, but they can drink water now too.

Crunch! Munch!

KEEPING CLEAN

Puppies are covered in **soft** fur.

While puppies are still young, their mother licks them to keep them clean. This is called grooming.

Slurp!

As they grow up, puppies learn how to **clean** themselves.

15

PLAY AND LEARN

Puppies love to **play!** Playing keeps them healthy and helps them learn how to run, chase, jump, catch and even fight.

Playing also teaches puppies about the world around them.

Splash!

Brrrr!

GROWING UP

As they grow up, puppies can look
after themselves better. At around two or three
months old, pet puppies are ready to leave
their mother and go to a new home.

Puppies keep
growing and changing
until they are about
a year old. At
six months old,
they get a new,
adult coat of fur.

19

A GROWN-UP DOG

By the time they reach their first birthday, almost all puppies are fully grown.

They are now called **dogs**.

Grown-up dogs can have puppies of their own.
They still love to **play** though!

A DOG'S LIFE CYCLE

newborn

Two months old

Four months old

A grown-up dog

22

fur

grooming

WORD BANK

solid food

newborn

teats

INDEX

Franklin Watts
First published in Great Britain in 2016
by The Watts Publishing Group

Copyright © The Watts Publishing Group 2016

All rights reserved.

Series Editor: Julia Bird
Series Designer: Basement 68

Picture credits: Nancy Dressel/Dreamstime: 14–15, 23tr.
Robert Fesus/Shutterstock: 1tr, 13, 23cr. Fnsy/Shutterstock:
8–9. Carson Ganci/Alamy: 18. Vaness Grossemy/Alamy:
front cover. Simon Hart/Alamy: 4–5, 24. Eric Isselee/
Shutterstock: 19, 22tr, 22br, 23tl. Rita Kochmarjova/
Shutterstock: 21. Sergey Lavrentev/Dreamstime: 6, 23cl.
Life on white/Alamy: 1bl, 10, 11. limitedqstock/Alamy: 17.
Luffmorgan/Dreamstime: 16. Marina Olena/Shutterstock:
7. Harry Page/Alamy: 2–3, 23b. Susan Smitz/Shutterstock:
12, 20. stockphoto mania/Shutterstock: 22tl. Umkehrer/
Shutterstock: 22bl.

Every attempt has been made to clear copyright.
Should there be any inadvertent omission please
apply to the publisher for rectification.

ISBN 978 1 4451 4835 9

Printed in China

MIX
Paper from
responsible sources
FSC
www.fsc.org   FSC® C104740

Franklin Watts
An imprint of
Hachette Children's Group
Part of The Watts Publishing Group
Carmelite House
50 Victoria Embankment
London EC4Y 0DZ

An Hachette UK Company
www.hachette.co.uk

www.franklinwatts.co.uk